The
Adventures of Sister Bernice

Touched By Greatness

Book 1

By

Koryn Philo

Dedication

To God, whose grace carried me through this journey.

To myself, for finding the courage to believe I could do it again.

And to my family and my publisher, Amanda, thank you for being the foundation that made this second milestone possible.

Table of Contents

Chapter 1

The Church of Cinnamon Rolls

Sister Bernice was a woman of deep faith—so deep, in fact, that she didn't feel the need to go to church every Sunday. Oh, no. Bernice wasn't your average church woman who required a hard wooden pew, a drafty sanctuary, and three hymns just to feel the Lord's presence.

She had a better idea. She had a system.

It was 5:45 in the morning. Outside, the streetlights of their suburban cul-de-sac were still humming, and the rest of the world was asleep. But inside the house, a low, rhythmic thumping bass was already vibrating the floorboards.

Down in the den, Leroy was awake. He was always awake. Bernice's husband of eighteen years was an early riser, but not for the reasons most men his age were. He wasn't checking the stock market or going for a jog. Leroy was huddled over a mixing board, headphones on, head bobbing to the beat of his latest hip-hop creation. He was in his zone, surrounded by monitors and wires, convinced that this snare drum was going to be the one that made him a legend.

Upstairs, Bernice rolled over and slapped her alarm clock before it could even think about buzzing. She swung her legs out of bed, slid her feet into her fuzzy slippers, and tightened the belt of her robe like she was preparing for battle.

She didn't head for the treadmill. She headed for the kitchen.

Bernice walked past the den, pausing just long enough to see the glow of Leroy's computer screen reflecting off his glasses. She shook her head lovingly. "Man's gonna turn into a subwoofer one of these days," she muttered to herself.

She entered the kitchen, the true heart of the home, and immediately retrieved her most essential spiritual tool: her iPad.

Bernice propped the tablet up against the flour jar and tapped the screen with a determined finger. She wasn't looking for recipes. She wasn't checking the weather. She was scrolling through looking for Joel Osteen or Seeds Of Greatness sermons, Yep her day wasn't complete without listening to one of them after her morning prayer devotions.

"Why go to church when you can bring church to you?" she whispered, pressing play.

As she listened in the kitchen—rich, booming, and full of conviction—Bernice got to work. This was her sanctuary. The smell of yeast and sugar began to rise as she kneaded the dough for her famous cinnamon rolls. She didn't care about the traditional Sunday routine of dressing up in hats and heels. She was "blessed with convenience."

She poured herself an extra cup of coffee, black, and took a sip just as the organ music swelled on the tablet.

"Preach, Pastor!!" she shouted, pointing a sticky, dough-covered finger at the screen.

Down the hall, the sound of sleepy groans emerged. The grandkids. All seventeen of them weren't living there, thank the Lord, but on weekends, it certainly felt like it. A pile of them crashed out in the living room on air mattresses, and Bernice knew that within the hour, the house would transform from a sanctuary of worship into a battleground over who got the last slice of cold pizza and whose turn it was on the Xbox.

But for now, it was just Bernice, The Pastor , and the dough.

Leroy wandered into the kitchen a few minutes later, scratching his head and blinking against the bright overhead lights. He pulled one side of his headphones off his ear.

"Bernice," he grumbled, his voice thick with sleep and skepticism. "Do we have to have the Holy Ghost in here at volume ten before the sun is even up? I'm trying to mix a track."

Bernice didn't look up. She was busy rolling out a sheet of dough with the precision of an architect. "Leroy, you make your noise, I make mine. The difference is my noise gets you into Heaven. Yours just wakes up the neighbors."

Leroy leaned against the counter, eyeing the tray of cinnamon rolls she was prepping. "Yeah,

well, if your cinnamon rolls didn't smell like glory, I'd lodge a formal complaint."

Bernice smirked, waving her spatula in the air like a church fan. "You can lodge a complaint with the management," she said, pointing a thumb toward the ceiling. "But I think he prefers my baking to your beats."

Leroy chuckled, a deep, belly laugh that warmed the room more than the oven did. He walked over, kissed her on the cheek, and swiped a pinch of raw dough before she could swat his hand away. "You keep telling yourself that, old woman. Just don't burn the kitchen down. You know I'm the only one in this house with fire extinguisher knowledge."

"I have never burned a roll in my life, Leroy. That is blasphemy."

He retreated to the coffeepot, pouring himself a mug. "So, what's the plan today? You gonna feed the five thousand with these rolls, or are we actually gonna have a quiet Saturday?"

Bernice paused. She looked at the rolls, then at her iPad, and then out the window where the sun was finally cracking the horizon. A familiar gleam entered her eye—a sparkle that Leroy had come to fear over the last two decades. It was the look of a woman who had just had an Idea.

She dusted the flour off her hands and leaned against the counter, spatula raised like a scepter.

"You know, Leroy," she said, her voice dropping to a conspiratorial whisper. "I was listening to the sermon yesterday... well, right now... and the Pastor said something about 'multiplying your talents.'"

Leroy froze, mug halfway to his mouth. "Bernice. No."

"I'm just saying," she continued, ignoring him completely. "These cinnamon rolls? They aren't just food. They're a ministry. People need comfort, Leroy. And what's more comforting than sugar and butter prayed over by a righteous woman?"

"Bernice," Leroy warned, "we still have three hundred 'Heavenly Handbags' in the garage from your last 'ministry.' I can't park my car."

"That was an inventory issue," she dismissed, waving the spatula again. "This is different. This is consumption. Consumable goods! It's the perfect business model!"

Leroy sighed, shaking his head as he walked back toward his den. "I'm going back to my studio. If the bank calls, tell them I moved to Mexico."

"Go ahead!" Bernice called after him. "But when I'm a tycoon, don't come asking for a loan for your new speakers!"

She turned back to her iPad, where the choir was now singing a high note. Bernice joined in, humming along as she popped the tray into the oven. She didn't know exactly what the business was going to be yet—maybe a delivery service, maybe a franchise—but she knew one thing.

She was Bernice. She had a spatula, she had a vision, and she had WIFI. The Lord was going to give her a sign, and until He did, she had cinnamon rolls to bake.

Chapter 2

A History of Hustle

By 8:00 A.M., the house was no longer a sanctuary; it was a zoo.

The smell of cinnamon rolls had done its job, acting as a sugary siren song that roused the sleeping giants from the living room. Seventeen grandkids—or at least the seven who were staying over that weekend—shuffled into the kitchen like zombies in pajamas.

"Mommom, is that the icing with the cream cheese or just the regular sugar kind?" asked Malik, the oldest at sixteen, rubbing sleep from his eyes.

"It's the *Blessed* kind," Bernice declared, sliding a fresh tray onto the cooling rack. "And before you touch a single crumb, wash those hands. I don't want your morning breath fingers on my inventory."

"Inventory?" Malik groaned, exchanging a look with his cousin, Tasha. "Oh no. She's doing it again."

Bernice ignored them, her mind already racing at a hundred miles an hour. To the untrained eye, she was just a grandmother feeding her family. But Bernice knew the truth: she was a CEO in a bathrobe, and this kitchen was her boardroom.

She wasn't just a listener of the Word; she was a doer. A mastermind. And like any great mastermind, she had a portfolio. A very… diverse portfolio.

Her grandkids settled around the kitchen island, arguing over who was going to get the center roll (the softest one) and whose turn it was to play the new *Call of Duty*. Bernice leaned against the sink, watching them.

"You know," she announced, her voice cutting through the debate about kill-streaks, "this batch right here represents a pivot in my business strategy."

The room went silent. Tasha dropped her head into her hands. "Mommom, please. Not before breakfast."

"I'm just saying!" Bernice waved a spatula. "You name it, I've tried it. And one of these days,

it's going to stick."

It was true. Bernice had a business plan for everything. Her resume of entrepreneurial ventures was long, colorful, and stored mostly in the garage, much to Leroy's dismay.

First, there was **Bernice's Blessed Baking**. It was a solid concept—cookies, cakes, and prayer-themed pies. The "Resurrection Raisin Pie" had been a hit at the church potluck, but the business model fell apart when Bernice realized she was eating more profits than she was selling.

Then came **Bernice's Blessings and Baskets**. She'd spent three months curating gift baskets filled with essential oils, inspirational quotes printed on cardstock, and—naturally—mini cinnamon rolls. That venture ended when the essential oils leaked onto the rolls, making the pastries taste like lavender and regret.

But Bernice wasn't a quitter. Oh no.

She pivoted to fashion with **Heavenly Handbags**. The tagline? *Carry the Lord with you.* They were purses with scriptures printed on the lining. "For the woman who wants to feel close to God, but also fashionable," she had pitched to her family.

"Mommom," Malik had said back then, "nobody wants to open their purse to find their lipstick and see 'Thou Shalt Not Steal' staring back at them."

"It's a theft deterrent!" Bernice had argued.

And let's not forget the cozy disaster that was **Bernice's Bibles and Blankets**. A combination of comfort and scripture, perfect for a cozy evening of prayer (or napping—depending on the day). That one actually showed promise, until the summer heatwave hit and nobody wanted a wool blanket, holy or otherwise.

"This could be my calling!" she'd shout with excitement every time a new idea struck.

Sitting at the island now, Malik bit into a cinnamon roll and looked at her with love, but also with deep exhaustion. "Mommom, you said that last time when you were selling the Miracle Garden Tools."

The kitchen erupted in giggles. Even Bernice had to fight back a smile.

"That was a legitimate product!" she defended.

"They were regular rakes from the dollar store," Tasha pointed out, laughing. "You just painted the handles gold and told people they only worked if you prayed over the weeds first."

"Well," Bernice said, lifting her chin with a blank, serious look. "Sometimes God's miracles

need a little… help. If you don't have faith, the weeds don't move. That's just science."

Her family was her focus group, her board of directors, and her toughest critics. Her three brothers and one beautiful sister, Darlene, were always there to support her, too—mostly.

Darlene often joked that she was going to set up a GoFundMe just to recoup the losses from Bernice's start-up costs. "I'm investing in your retirement, Bernice," Darlene would say, sipping tea on the porch. "Or at least, I'm investing in keeping Leroy from having a stroke when he sees the credit card bill."

Her brothers were simpler men. They would nod along as she pitched her latest "niche," eating her food with enthusiasm. "You can never have too many businesses," her brother Earl would say with a mouthful of brisket. "And I'm just here for the barbecue."

But her parents... they were the best. They would sit on the porch, hands folded, looking at her in amazement, always with a loving smile.

"Bernice, honey," her mother would say, "you've got so many ideas. What are you really trying to do?"

"Find my niche, Mommy," Bernice would reply with absolute confidence. "I'm this close. I can feel it. I'm just waiting on God to give me the green light."

Back in the kitchen, the chaos of the grandkids had returned to full volume. The cinnamon rolls were vanishing. The arguments about video games had resumed.

Bernice turned back to the window. She was taking online courses now. She was reading business books with titles like *The Monk Who Sold His Ferrari* and *The Grandma Who Sold Her Knits*. She was even having deep spiritual discussions with the cashiers at the local grocery store, testing out taglines on women just trying to buy milk.

She had briefly considered a "Divine Date Night" service—complete with candles, Christian romance novels, and prayer circles—until Malik had pointed out that she might be attracting "the weird kind of clientele" to her church-led matchmaking business.

She wasn't bothered. Not really.

"Go ahead and laugh," she told the grandkids, wiping down the counter. "But when I launch this subscription box for Christian motivation... or maybe Bible Karaoke..."

"Bible Karaoke?" Tasha choked on her juice. "Sing praises and work out at the same time?" "Exactly!" Bernice beamed. "Sweat for the Savior! It's a goldmine!"

She looked over at the empty tray of cinnamon rolls. Not a crumb left.

Her life may have seemed like one long search for the perfect business idea, but Bernice knew something others didn't: life was a journey. She might not have found her exact "purpose" yet, but she was getting closer.

Every grandkid she fed, every roll she baked, and every sermon she streamed was part of the divine R&D department.

"Mommom?" Malik asked, standing up and dusting sugar off his shirt. "Can I borrow five dollars?"

Bernice narrowed her eyes. "For what?"

"Investment capital," he grinned. "For my video game empire."

Bernice reached into her robe pocket and pulled out a crumpled bill. "I expect a return on this investment, young man. We are a family of entrepreneurs."

She watched them scatter toward the living room, the sugar fueling their energy. She might not have gone to a church building this morning, but looking at her loud, happy, chaotic family, she felt pretty close to Heaven anyway.

Now, if she could just figure out how to monetize it.

Chapter 3

The Divine Date Night Disaster

If you asked Leroy, the most dangerous phrase in the English language wasn't "fire in the hole" or "IRS audit." It was Bernice standing in the middle of the living room, hands on her hips, saying, "I have a vision."

And nothing proved his point quite like the incident of the "Divine Date Night."

It had happened a few months prior, during a lull between the "Bibles and Blankets" phase and the "Holy Hummus" experiment. Bernice had decided that the singles in her community weren't suffering from a lack of options; they were suffering from a lack of *sanctified atmosphere*.

"People don't know how to court anymore, Leroy," she had insisted, dragging the coffee table out of the living room to make space for two folding chairs. "It's all swiping left and swiping right. No dignity. No spirit."

"So your plan is to turn our living room into a matchmaking service?" Leroy had asked, watching from the safety of his recliner. "Bernice, I live here. I walk around in my boxers here."

"Not tonight you don't," she had snapped. "Tonight, you are the ambience coordinator."

The business model for **Divine Date Night** was simple: Bernice would provide a "God-honoring romantic environment" for couples to get to know each other, complete with a three-course meal, chaperoned conversation, and intercessory prayer.

For her beta test, she had practically kidnapped two single people she knew vaguely from the neighborhood. There was Brother Marcus, a shy man who worked at the post office, and Sister Clara, a woman Bernice had met in the produce aisle who seemed to really enjoy squeezing cantaloupes.

Bernice had transformed the living room. She draped lace doilies over every available surface. She set up a card table with her best China. And, to set the mood, she deployed no fewer than forty battery-operated tea lights.

"It looks like a shrine in here, Bernice," Leroy had whispered, peeking out from the kitchen. "Are we dating them or burying them?"

"Hush," Bernice hissed, adjusting a bowl of potpourri. "It's romantic."

When Marcus and Clara arrived, looking terrified and clutching their purses and wallets like they were being held for ransom, Bernice went into full Matriarch Mode.

"Welcome to Divine Date Night," she announced, ushering them in. "Tonight is about connection. Connection with each other, and connection with the Word."

She sat them down at the card table, which was so small their knees were practically locked together. She served them her signature meatloaf, but before they could take a bite, she slammed a deck of index cards onto the table.

"We don't do small talk here," Bernice declared. "We do *Deep Dives*. Pick a card."

Marcus, trembling slightly, picked a card. He read it aloud. "*If you were a biblical plague, which one would you be and why?*"

Silence filled the room. The tea lights flickered.

"I... uh..." Marcus stammered. "Locusts?"

Clara stared at him. "Locusts? Really? I'm more of a frog person."

From the kitchen, Leroy let out a snort of laughter he tried to disguise as a cough.

But the real disaster struck during the "Entertainment Portion." Bernice had decided that instead of music or a movie, the couple would enjoy a dramatic reading of a Christian romance novel she had picked up at a thrift store.

She stood by the fireplace (which was actually just a TV screen playing a video of a fireplace)

and began to read.

"*He looked at her with eyes full of redemption,*" Bernice read with theatrical flair, "*and whispered, 'Mildred, your faith is as strong as a cedar of Lebanon.*'"

Marcus was sweating. Clara was checking her watch.

"Okay, now," Bernice said, clapping the book shut. "Hold hands. It's time for the prayer circle." "The... what?" Clara asked, looking ready to bolt.

"We have to seal the date with prayer!" Bernice insisted. She grabbed their hands, forcing them into a triangle of awkwardness. "Lord, we ask that you bind these two together! Let them find a niche in each other's hearts! Let their love be profitable and their spirits be... coordinated!"

Just then, the front door opened.

It was Malik, coming home from basketball practice with two of his friends. They stopped dead in their tracks. They took in the scene: the forty flickering candles, the lace doilies, the terrified couple holding hands with their grandmother, and Leroy in the corner shaking his head.

"Whoa," Malik said, eyes wide. "Mommom... is this a séance?"

"It's a date!" Bernice shouted.

"It looks like you're summoning the ghost of relationships past," Malik cracked.

Marcus took the opportunity to stand up. "I... I think I left my oven on. At home. Ideally, I should go check that."

"Me too," Clara said, grabbing her purse. "I also left his oven on."

They fled the house faster than the Israelites fled Egypt.

Bernice stood amidst the fake candles, holding a meatloaf pan. She looked at the empty table, then at Leroy.

"Well," she said, undeterred. "Maybe the market isn't ready for that level of intimacy yet."

Leroy walked over, picked up a tea light, and turned it off. "Bernice, baby," he said, putting an arm around her. "I think you might have the market cornered on 'scaring people away.' That wasn't a date. That was a hostage situation with gravy."

Bernice pouted for exactly three seconds before she shrugged. "Fine. It was more about the

dinner anyway. They missed out on some good meatloaf."

"I didn't," Leroy said, grabbing a fork. "Pass the plate. And turn off the fake fireplace. It's making me hot."

As Bernice cleaned up the "shrine" later that night, she didn't feel defeated. She felt refined.

"You know, Leroy," she called out as she blew out the last candle. "I think the problem wasn't the idea. It was the branding. Maybe next time, less candles, more... cinnamon."

Leroy, mouth full of meatloaf, just shook his head. "Please, Bernice. No more dating. Stick to things that don't have a pulse."

"We'll see," she whispered to herself. "We'll see."

Chapter 4

Two Sides of the Same Coin

If marriage is a dance, Bernice and Leroy were doing two completely different routines to two different songs, yet somehow, they never stepped on each other's toes.

They were the definition of "opposites attract." Bernice was a woman of grand, sweeping gestures. She lived her life in bold font, italicized, with exclamation points. She filled rooms with the scent of yeast, the sound of gospel choirs, and the chaotic energy of a woman who believed her next million-dollar idea was just one spatula wave away.

Leroy, on the other hand, was the baseline. He was the steady, rhythmic thump of a kick drum. While Bernice was vibrating at a high frequency of spiritual entrepreneurship, Leroy was cool, sarcastic, and pragmatic. He was a man who read the instruction manual before assembling the furniture. Bernice was a woman who prayed over the box and hoped the screws would find their own way home.

Their disagreements were legendary, though they rarely rose above the volume of a spirited debate.

"Bernice," Leroy said one Tuesday evening, leaning against the doorframe of the kitchen. He held a piece of paper in his hand. "Why is there a charge on the credit card for 'Holy Hydroponics'?"

Bernice didn't look up from the cutting board, where she was aggressively dicing bell peppers. "That is R&D, Leroy. Research and

Development. I'm looking into growing biblical herbs. Hyssop, Leroy. Do you know the market value of fresh hyssop?"

"I don't," Leroy deadpanned. "And I don't think the electric company accepts hyssop as payment."

"Ye of little faith," she muttered, sliding the peppers into a sizzling pan. "You're just grumpy because your snare drum sound isn't 'snappy' enough."

Leroy cracked a smile. She had him there. He had been complaining about a snare sample for three days.

"My snare is fine," he said, walking over to the fridge. "It's crisp. Unlike this financial strategy."

He grabbed a bottle of water, but instead of leaving, he set it down. He washed his hands, picked up a knife, and silently moved to the other side of the island. Without asking, he grabbed a bag of onions and started chopping.

This was their rhythm. For all his talk about her "putting them in the poor house," Leroy was always right there, in the trenches. He was her unspoken sous-chef.

"You're cutting those too thick," Bernice critiqued, glancing at his pile.

"I'm cutting them for texture, woman," Leroy shot back, not breaking his rhythm. "You want flavor? You need surface area. I'm applying audio engineering principles to these onions."

Bernice rolled her eyes, but she couldn't hide the smile tugging at the corner of her mouth. "Just don't cry on my produce. I don't need salty onions."

"I only cry when I look at our bank statement," he retorted.

They worked in comfortable silence for a moment, the only sounds the *chop-chop-chop* of the knife and the bubbling of the pot.

"You know," Leroy said after a moment, "I'm the only reason this house is still standing. You get to cooking and thinking about your next business, and you forget you have an open flame on the stove."

"I have never started a fire," Bernice lied.

"Bernice, the 'Burning Bush Barbecue' incident of 2018? The fire department came. They knew you by name."

"That was a malfunction of the equipment," she sniffed. "And the ribs were still delicious."

"The ribs were charcoal," Leroy laughed, a deep, resonant sound. "I'm just saying. I'm the safety officer in this operation. I'm the one with the fire extinguisher knowledge. You bring the heat; I bring the foam."

"You bring the hot air," she corrected, bumping his hip with hers.

He bumped her back, harder. "Watch it. Or I'll go on strike, and you'll have to chop these

onions yourself."

"You wouldn't dare. You know you love my cooking too much."

"It's true," he admitted, scraping the onions into the pot. "You're a headache, Bernice, but you feed me well."

Later that night, the dynamic shifted.

The kitchen was clean—well, mostly clean—and the house had settled into its nighttime hum. Bernice was on the couch, a fuzzy blanket draped over her lap, a notebook open as she sketched out a logo for *Sister Bernice's Sanctified Smoothies*.

Leroy was in his corner of the living room, headphones on, head bobbing. The soft blue light of his laptop illuminated his face, highlighting the gray in his beard. He looked focused, peaceful.

Bernice stopped sketching. She watched him. She loved the way his brow furrowed when he was tweaking a bassline. She loved that even after eighteen years, he still had dreams of his own.

She tossed a throw pillow at him. It hit his shoulder with a soft *thud*.

Leroy pulled one ear cup off. "What? Did you invent a new currency?"

"Let me hear it," she said softly.

Leroy hesitated. He was protective of his beats. They were his diary. But he unplugged the headphones.

A smooth, jazzy hip-hop track filled the room. It was soulful, complex, and a little melancholy. It sounded like a rainy Sunday morning.

Bernice closed her eyes, listening. She tapped her foot beneath the blanket. "That's good, Leroy," she said after a minute. "That's really good. It sounds like... patience." Leroy looked at her, surprised. "Patience?"

"Yeah. Like waiting for something good to happen." She opened her eyes and smiled at him. "You're talented, old man. Don't let nobody tell you different."

Leroy smiled, a genuine, unguarded smile that took ten years off his face. "Thanks, B. Maybe one day they'll call me Leroy the Beatmaker. The man who brought rhythm to the suburbs."

"They better," she said, picking up her pen again. "Because one of us has to be famous. And if

my *Sanctified Smoothies* don't take off, it's all on you."

"Great," Leroy sighed, plugging his headphones back in. "No pressure." "I'll pray for you," Bernice said, squeezing his knee as he sat down next to her on the couch.

"And I'll pray for me, too," he muttered, opening a new track. "Mostly that you don't buy a blender for those smoothies."

They sat there for another hour, side by side. Him making music, her building empires in a notebook. They were night and day, fire and foam, beats and baking. But in the quiet of the living room, they fit together perfectly.

Chapter 5

The Kitchen Alchemist

Sister Bernice was a woman of mystery, and her kitchen was the sacred grove where the magic happened.

In a world obsessed with precision—with measuring cups, digital scales, and instructions that insisted you "level the teaspoon"—Bernice was a rebel. She didn't believe in recipes. She believed in *vibes*. She believed in the Holy Spirit guiding her hand toward the paprika.

"How much salt did you put in that?" her daughter-in-law had asked once, watching Bernice season a pot of collard greens.

"Enough," Bernice had replied, not even looking at the pot. "You stop shaking when your ancestors whisper *'that's good, child.'*"

On this particular Wednesday, the kitchen was quiet. The grandkids were at school, and Leroy was in the living room, the soft *thump-thump-hiss* of a new beat drifting through the doorway.

Bernice stood before the kitchen island, staring down a bowl of romaine lettuce. It looked sad. It looked uninspired. It looked like it needed a revival.

"I just took some things out," she muttered to herself, opening the fridge door and scanning the shelves. "I'll figure it out when I get it in the bowl… oh boy, or oh boy!"

She started grabbing bottles. Olive oil. Apple cider vinegar. A jar of Dijon mustard that had been in the back since Easter. A lemon that looked like it had seen better days.

Leroy wandered in, lured by the sound of jars clinking. He leaned against the doorframe, crossing his arms.

"What is it today, Bernice?" he asked, eyeing the chaotic spread of ingredients. "We doing 'Sanctified Stew'? 'Pentecostal Pasta'?"

"It's salad, Leroy," she said, uncorking the vinegar. "But it's missing... the anointing."

"The anointing," Leroy repeated. "Right. Bernice, I've seen you 'toss things together' before. Remember the 'Manna Mashed Potatoes'? They were burnt, yet somehow tasted like glory. It was confusing."

"That was a texture choice," she dismissed him, grabbing a whisk. "Now hush. I'm creating."

She began to pour. She didn't measure. A glug of oil. A splash of vinegar. A scoop of mustard. She reached into her spice cabinet and grabbed a handful of green herbs—oregano? Basil? Parsley? She didn't know, and frankly, she didn't care. Into the bowl they went.

She whisked furiously, her wrist moving with the speed of a hummingbird. She dipped a pinky finger in. She tasted it. She frowned.

"It's good," she murmured, smacking her lips. "But it's missing something. It needs... a zing. A testimony."

Leroy shook his head, walking over to inspect the bowl. "There's always a zing with you, Bernice. Maybe just add salt like a normal person?"

"Salt is for the common man, Leroy. This needs elevation."

She scanned the counter. Her eyes landed on a golden bear-shaped bottle.

"Honey!" she gasped. "Sweetness! That's what it needs. To balance the bitterness of life... and the vinegar."

"Bernice, don't put honey in the salad dressing," Leroy warned. "That's gonna be weird." "Watch me."

She squeezed the bear. A generous, unmeasured stream of gold spiraled into the mixture. She whisked again. The dressing changed color, thickening into a creamy, golden emulsion that caught the light from the window.

Bernice dipped her finger in again.

Her eyes went wide. She froze.

"Oh," she whispered. "Oh my."

"What?" Leroy asked, stepping closer. "Did you poison yourself?"

She shoved her finger toward his face. "Taste this, Leroy. Taste the victory."

Leroy hesitated, then dipped his own finger into the bowl. He tasted it. He paused. He tasted it again, just to be sure.

The flavors hit him all at once—the sharp tang of the vinegar, the heat of the mustard, the savory herbs, and then, right at the end, that smooth, perfect ribbon of honey tying it all together. It wasn't just good. It was *addictive.*

"Okay," Leroy admitted, looking at the bowl with newfound respect. "That... that is actually hitting."

"Hitting?" Bernice scoffed. "Leroy, this is singing. This is a choir in a bottle."

She grabbed a piece of lettuce, dipped it, and ate it with her eyes closed. "I know what I'm going to call it."

Leroy groaned. "Here we go. What? 'Holy Honey Mustard'?"

"No," she said, opening her eyes with fierce determination. "I'm going to call it... **Touch My Greatness**."

Leroy choked on his own spit. "Touch *My* Greatness? Bernice, no. That sounds... illegal. Or at least like a lawsuit waiting to happen."

"Why?" she asked, innocent as a dove. "It's great. And I touched it."

"It sounds like a memoir nobody wants to read," Leroy countered. "Change it."

Bernice thought for a moment, tapping the whisk against her chin. "Fine. How about... **Touch By Greatness**?"

Leroy tilted his head. "Touch *By* Greatness. Okay. That's better. Sounds like you're selling a superpower in a bottle."

"I am Leroy!" she laughed, grabbing a mason jar and pouring the liquid gold inside. "This dressing is about to change the world. It's not just for salads. It'll go on everything. Chicken! Vegetables! Tacos! Even... pizza!"

"Don't put it on pizza, Bernice. You're crossing a line."

"I'm erasing lines, Leroy! I'm an innovator!"

She screwed the lid onto the jar and held it up to the light. It glowed.

"Touch By Greatness," she whispered. "The Dressing That Will Bless Your Taste Buds." Leroy walked back to the living room, shaking his head, but he was smiling. "I gotta admit,

Bernice," he called back over his shoulder. "You figured it out. Again."

"I always do!" she shouted back, already reaching for another empty jar. "Now get out of my office! I have to scale up production!"

Leroy sat back down at his computer, but before he put his headphones on, he looked toward the kitchen. He could hear her humming a hymn, the sound of jars clinking, and the frantic whisking of a woman who had just stumbled upon her destiny.

"Touch By Greatness," he muttered to himself, chuckling. "She's actually gonna do it." He opened a new audio file and renamed it: *The Dressing Theme Song - Draft 1*. Bernice had the sauce. Now, he just needed to give it a beat.

Chapter 6

The Soft Launch

Bernice didn't believe in focus groups. She didn't believe in market research. She believed in the "Glenda Test."

Glenda was the cashier at aisle four of the Super-Save grocery store. Glenda had bad bunions, a skeptical outlook on life, and a scanning speed that defied the laws of physics. If you could sell Glenda on an idea between the scanning of the milk and the bagging of the eggs, you had a hit.

It was Tuesday morning, three days after the invention of *Touch By Greatness*. Bernice stood at the register, her cart overflowing with olive oil, Dijon mustard, and enough honey to put a bear into a diabetic coma.

"That's a lot of oil, Sister Bernice," Glenda droned, sliding the bottles across the scanner. *Beep. Beep. Beep.* "You frying a turkey or lubricating a slip-n-slide?"

"Neither, Glenda," Bernice said, leaning over the check-writing pad conspiratorially. "I'm manufacturing blessings."

She reached into her oversized purse—one of the leftover *Heavenly Handbags* with 'Rejoice!' embroidered on the strap—and pulled out a mason jar. The liquid inside glowed amber gold. The label was a standard Avery address label, on which Bernice had written in sharpie: *TOUCH BY GREATNESS.*

"Here," Bernice said, sliding the jar onto the conveyor belt next to a pack of gum. "It's on the house."

Glenda eyed the jar suspiciously. "What is it? Moonshine?"

"It's salad dressing, Glenda. But it's also an anointing oil for your insides. Put it on your kale. Put it on your chicken. Put it on your bunions if they act up—though I can't legally claim it heals feet yet."

Glenda picked up the jar, shook it, and shrugged. "Free is my favorite flavor. I'll try it." "You won't just try it, honey. You'll be transformed."

Bernice left the store with a spring in her step. Phase One was complete. By Friday, Phase Two—"The Neighborhood Blitz"—was in full swing.

Bernice treated the distribution of her product like a reverse burglary. She would creep up to neighbors' porches, look left and right, and leave a jar of dressing on the welcome mat with a note that simply read: *You're Welcome - Sister B.*

The mailman, Mr. Henderson, wasn't safe either. He walked up the driveway to deliver a stack of bills, and Bernice met him at the door before he could even ring the bell.

"Morning, Mr. Henderson!" she chirped, shoving a jar into his hand. "Hydrate your soul!"

"Bernice, I just have a package for Leroy," he stammered, holding the jar like a grenade. "Is this... soup?"

"It's whatever you need it to be, baby. Just shake it before you pour it."

For forty-eight hours, the house was quiet. Leroy assumed the craze had passed, just like the essential oils had passed. He sat in his den, working on a remix, enjoying the peace.

Then, the phone started ringing.

"Hello?" Bernice answered the landline in the kitchen.

"Bernice!" It was Glenda. She didn't sound bored anymore. She sounded frantic. "Girl, what was in that jar? I put it on a pork chop last night, and my husband—who hasn't complimented my cooking since the Reagan administration—asked for seconds. I need three more jars. My sister is coming to town."

Bernice smiled. "Praise Him."

Ten minutes later, there was a knock at the door. It was Mrs. Gable from next door. She was holding an empty jar and looking desperate.

"Bernice," she whispered, "I drank the last bit straight from the jar. Don't judge me. I just need a refill. I have a potluck tonight and I need to win."

By Sunday evening, the Bernice & Leroy residence had transformed. It was no longer a home; it was a bottling plant.

Every surface in the kitchen was covered. There were gallons of vinegar on the floor. There were crates of mason jars stacked on the dining room table. The smell of garlic and mustard hung in the air so thick you could chew it.

Leroy walked out of his den, empty coffee mug in hand, and stopped dead in his tracks.

He tried to walk to the sink, but his path was blocked by a tower of empty honey bears. He turned to the pantry, but the door wouldn't open—it was blocked by boxes of shipping labels.

"Bernice," Leroy said, his voice dangerously calm.

"Yes, sugar?" Bernice was at the island, wearing a hairnet and an apron, whisking a bowl the size of a tire.

"Why is there a crate of paprika on my subwoofer?"

Bernice didn't look up. "We ran out of counter space. Adapt and overcome, Leroy. That subwoofer is now the Spice Zone."

"The Spice Zone?" Leroy rubbed his temples. "Bernice, I can't make beats in a warehouse. The acoustics are terrible. And I smell like a vinaigrette."

"You smell like success," she corrected. "Do you know how many orders we got today? Twelve! That's twelve jars, Leroy. At eight dollars a pop!"

"Eight dollars?" Leroy did the math. "That's... ninety-six dollars."

"It's a fortune!" Bernice cheered. "We are practically moguls!"

"Bernice, the gas to drive to the store cost more than ninety-six dollars," Leroy sighed, moving a stack of labels so he could reach the coffee pot. "And we are running out of jars. I saw you washing out an old mayonnaise jar earlier. That's low class."

"It's upcycling! It's eco-friendly!"

"It's Hellmann's, Bernice. You can't sell God's greatness in a Hellmann's jar."

Leroy grumbled as he poured his coffee, but as he turned to leave, he saw the list of orders taped to the fridge. It wasn't just Glenda and Mrs. Gable anymore. There were names he didn't know. *Pastor Miller. The Deacon Board. That lady from the bank.*

He looked at Bernice. She was tired. There was flour on her nose (though why she was using flour for salad dressing, he didn't know—it was her secret) and a wild look in her eyes. But she

looked happy. Happier than she had been in years.

He sighed, walked over to the "Spice Zone," and picked up the crate of paprika. "I'm moving this to the garage," he announced. "My subwoofer is for bass, not basil."

"Thank you, Leroy!" she called out. "And while you're out there, bring in those empty boxes! We have shipping to do!"

Leroy walked to the garage, muttering to himself. "Seventeen grandkids, three brothers, and I'm the one moving paprika."

But as he set the crate down, he found himself humming. It was a catchy melody. Something upbeat. Something that sounded like... dressing.

"Touch By Greatness," he sang softly to the rhythm of his footsteps. "Yeah. It's got a ring to it."

Back in the kitchen, Bernice poured another jar. The soft launch was over. The hard work—and the child labor she was about to recruit—was just beginning.

Chapter 7

The Grandkids' Rebellion

There is a specific sound that strikes fear into the heart of any grandchild under the age of eighteen. It isn't the sound of a belt snapping. It isn't the sound of thunder.

It is the sound of the front door deadbolt clicking *locked* behind you immediately after you walk into your grandmother's house on a Saturday.

Malik heard the click. He froze in the hallway, his backpack—filled with video games and controllers—still heavy on his shoulders. He looked at his cousin Tasha, who was standing beside him holding a sleepover bag.

"Did she just..." Tasha started.

"She locked it," Malik whispered. "We're trapped."

Sister Bernice emerged from the kitchen like a general stepping onto the battlefield. She wasn't holding a tray of cookies. She was holding a clipboard.

"Welcome, children!" she boomed, her smile a little too wide. "Welcome to the headquarters of Bernice Enterprises Global."

"Mommom," Malik said, taking a step back. "We just came to play *Fortnite* on PopPop's big TV. Mom said you were making pizza."

"Oh, there will be pizza," Bernice assured them, tapping the clipboard with a pen. "Pizza is for closers. Pizza is for laborers. Pizza is the fuel of the righteous."

She gestured grandly toward the dining room.

The grandkids peered around the corner. The dining room table—usually reserved for Thanksgiving and serious discussions about grades—had been transformed. It was covered in a plastic tarp. On top of the tarp sat three hundred empty mason jars, a stack of sticky labels, a vat of dressing, and a roll of twine.

"What is this?" Tasha asked, horrified.

"This," Bernice said, "is your inheritance. Or at least, the start of it. We have orders to fill, babies. The people are thirsty for Greatness, and we are the vessel."

"We?" Malik clarified.

"We," Bernice confirmed. "Now, put your bags down. Malik, you're pouring. You have steady hands from all that gaming. Tasha, you're on labeling. Keep them straight. The Lord loves a cheerful giver, but He also loves a level sticker."

The rebellion began immediately.

"Mommom, this is child labor," Tasha argued, crossing her arms. "I'm pretty sure this violates several international treaties. Or at least OSHA regulations."

"This isn't labor," Bernice scoffed. "This is an *internship*. An unpaid, family-based internship with high growth potential."

"Unpaid?" Malik's voice cracked. "Mommom, I need gas money. I can't pour dressing for exposure."

Bernice sighed, looking toward the ceiling as if asking for patience. "You kids today. Everything is a transaction. What happened to duty? What happened to helping your elders?"

"Inflation happened," Malik shot back. "Gas is four dollars a gallon."

Leroy walked by the hallway, holding a cup of coffee. He paused, looking at the standoff.

"She's got you there, Bernice," Leroy noted. "You can't pay them in wisdom. Wisdom doesn't buy sneakers."

Bernice narrowed her eyes at her husband. "Whose side are you on, Judas?"

"I'm on the side of the people," Leroy chuckled, retreating to his den. "Unionize, kids! Don't settle for pepperoni!"

Bernice turned back to the grandkids. They were standing their ground. Tasha actually had her phone out, probably looking up child labor laws.

Bernice knew when she was beaten. She was a businesswoman, after all. It was time to negotiate.

"Fine," Bernice said, dropping the clipboard. "Here is the offer. You work for four hours. We fill these three hundred jars. In exchange, I provide..."

"Fifty dollars," Malik cut in.

"Fifty dollars?" Bernice clutched her chest. "For pouring liquid? Are you a surgeon?"

"Fifty dollars each," Tasha added. "And the pizza has to be from the good place, not the frozen kind."

Bernice grimaced. "Thirty dollars each. And I make the pizza homemade. My dough is anointed."

"Forty," Malik countered. "Cash. Upfront. And we pick the music while we work."

Bernice hesitated. Forty dollars was a significant chunk of her profit margin. But she looked at the mountain of jars. She looked at her arthritic wrists. She looked at the determination in Malik's eyes—a determination that reminded her suspiciously of herself.

"Fine," she snapped. "Forty. But if I see one crooked label, Tasha, I'm docking your pay. And Malik, if you spill a drop of Greatness, it's coming out of your inheritance."

"Deal," they said in unison.

Ten minutes later, the dining room was a hive of activity. But it wasn't the silent, reverent atmosphere Bernice had envisioned.

Malik had connected his phone to the Bluetooth speaker. Instead of Bernice's preferred gospel hymns, the room was thumping with a heavy trap beat—one of Leroy's, actually, that he had uploaded to SoundCloud.

"This music is aggressive," Bernice complained, carefully funneling dressing into jars while Malik poured. "I feel like I'm jarring dressing in a nightclub."

"It helps the workflow, Mommmom," Malik said, bobbing his head. "Look at the rhythm. Pour, lid, twist. Pour, lid, twist."

Tasha was at the end of the table, slapping labels on with surprising speed. "So, Mommmom, what's the long-term plan here?" she asked. "Are we going public? Are you selling to Amazon?

Or is this just a trunk-of-the-car operation?"

Bernice looked at her granddaughter with surprise. "Look at you, using business words. I'm impressed. The plan is... expansion. Global domination. A bottle of Touch By Greatness on every table in America."

"You need a website," Tasha said flatly. "And Instagram. Nobody trusts a product they can't tag."

"I have a Facebook," Bernice defended. "I post on my wall."

"Mommmom, you post pictures of your thumb covering the lens," Tasha sighed. "I'll set up the Instagram. But that's extra. That's a consulting fee."

Bernice laughed. She couldn't help it. "You really are my grandbaby. Always looking for the angle."

"I learned from the best," Tasha smirked.

For the next four hours, they worked. The kitchen got messy. Tasha got dressing in her hair. Malik dropped a jar, which shattered and forced everyone to evacuate the "Hazard Zone" until Bernice mopped it up.

But they did it. Three hundred jars, filled, capped, and labeled.

As the sun began to set, they sat around the kitchen island, exhausted, eating the homemade pizza Bernice had promised. It was, as always, delicious.

"Not bad," Malik admitted, wiping tomato sauce from his lip. "We actually crushed that."

"We did," Bernice agreed, looking at the wall of boxed jars stacked by the door. She reached into her robe pocket and pulled out a wad of cash. She peeled off four twenties.

"Here," she said, handing them the money. "Don't spend it all on... whatever you buy. Skins? V-Bucks?"

"Thanks, Mommom," Malik said, pocketing the cash instantly.

Leroy wandered back into the kitchen, drawn by the smell of pepperoni. He looked at the finished jars, then at the tired grandkids.

"Well," Leroy said, grabbing a slice of pizza. "Looks like you didn't kill them, Bernice. I'm surprised."

"They have potential," Bernice nodded. "They're expensive, but they have potential."

She looked at her grandkids—sticky, tired, holding their cash—and felt a surge of pride. They might not understand her spiritual journey, and they might charge her union rates, but they were here.

"Same time next Saturday?" Bernice asked innocently.

Malik and Tasha looked at each other. They looked at the cash.

"Make it fifty," Malik said.

Bernice smiled. "We'll see."

Chapter 8

Cinnamon Roll Devotions

Lights. Camera. Anointing.

The kitchen island had been cleared of the salad dressing assembly line to make way for the new venture. Bernice stood in the center of the room, smoothing out her best floral apron. She had applied a little extra rouge for the occasion and was wearing a hat that could only be described as "architectural."

"Okay, production team," Bernice announced, clapping her flour-dusted hands. "Let's get a sound check."

The "production team" consisted of a very reluctant Leroy holding his iPhone and Tasha, who was sitting on a stool acting as the "Creative Director."

"Mommom, you don't need a sound check," Tasha said, scrolling through TikTok on her own phone. "You're loud enough to be heard in the next zip code without a microphone."

"It's called projection, Tasha," Bernice corrected. "It's a homiletic skill. Leroy, is the lighting adequate? Do I look radiant?"

Leroy squinted at the screen of his phone. "You look like you're standing in a kitchen, Bernice. Because you are. Can we hurry this up? I have a session at three."

"You can't rush the Spirit, Leroy. And you certainly can't rush yeast."

The concept was simple—at least in Bernice's head. It was called **Cinnamon Roll Devotions**. The tagline: *Sugar for the Body, Scripture for the Soul.* She would bake her famous rolls while delivering a mini-sermon about the trials of life. It was basically the Food Network meets the tent revival.

"Alright," Bernice said, taking a deep breath. "Action!"

Leroy tapped the record button. "Rolling."

Bernice smiled a smile that was 80% teeth and 20% terror. She looked directly into the camera lens.

"Welcome, saints and sinners!" she shouted.

"Cut," Leroy said immediately. "Too loud. You peaked the audio. You're in the red." Bernice frowned. "I was welcoming them! I have to be enthusiastic!"

"Be enthusiastic at a volume that doesn't blow out the speaker," Leroy advised. "Try again. Softer. Like you're talking to a friend."

"Take two," Tasha called out.

Bernice composed herself. She grabbed a rolling pin. She looked at the camera with intense, piercing eyes.

"Hello, friends," she whispered, sounding vaguely threatening. "Today, we are going to roll out the sin in our lives... just like this dough."

She slammed the rolling pin down onto the counter with a violent *THWACK*. "Whoa!" Leroy jumped. "Bernice, you trying to bake bread or assault it?" "I'm emphasizing the point, Leroy! Sin is stubborn! You have to beat it out!" "Okay, but maybe don't beat the counter so hard? The camera is shaking."

They tried again. And again. By Take 14, the dough was starting to get warm, and Bernice was sweating.

"This is harder than it looks," she admitted, wiping her brow with a forearm. "How do those people on TV do it? They chop onions and talk about their childhoods without crying."

"They have editors," Tasha said. "Just be yourself, Mommom. Stop trying to be the TV lady. Just be Mommom."

Bernice nodded. "Okay. Just me. Just Bernice."

"Take 15," Leroy sighed. "Action."

Bernice took a breath. She stopped looking at the camera and started looking at the dough. She began to knead it, her hands moving with the muscle memory of fifty years.

"You know," she started, her voice natural and rhythmic, "life gets tough. It gets sticky. Just

like this dough. Sometimes you feel like you're being pulled and stretched in a thousand directions. You got grandkids wanting money, a husband wanting attention, and bills wanting payment."

Leroy smiled behind the phone. *There it is.*

"But you gotta let it rise," Bernice continued, punching the dough gently. "You can't rush the rise. If you put it in the oven too soon, it's gonna be flat. It's gonna be hard. You gotta sit in the warmth and wait. That's where the flavor is. In the waiting."

She was on a roll. She grabbed the bowl of cinnamon sugar filling.

"And then," she preached, "you gotta add the sweetness. The grace. You sprinkle it on everything!"

She grabbed a handful of cinnamon sugar and tossed it with a little too much fervor. A cloud of brown dust exploded into the air.

"And then you roll it up tight!" Bernice shouted, getting excited again. She grabbed the edge of the dough. "You gotta roll with the punches! You gotta twist and shout!"

She waved her hands. Her elbow connected with the bag of flour standing open next to her. *POOF.*

A white mushroom cloud erupted, engulfing Bernice.

"Oh Lord!" she coughed, waving her hands blindly. "I'm in the cloud! I'm in the glory cloud!"

In her blindness, she reached out to stabilize herself. Her hand hit the tripod—a stack of cookbooks Leroy had rigged up to hold a secondary light. The books shifted. The light tipped. It hit Leroy's arm.

Leroy jerked. The phone slipped from his fingers.

It tumbled through the air in slow motion. Tasha gasped. Bernice froze. *SPLAT.*

The phone landed face-up, directly in the bowl of melted butter and egg wash. Silence filled the kitchen.

Bernice peered through the settling flour dust. She looked at the bowl. She looked at Leroy. "Leroy," she whispered. "Is that your phone?"

Leroy stared at the bowl. He walked over slowly. He picked up the phone by the corner. It was dripping with yellow goo. The screen was still on. It was still recording.

"Well," Leroy said, his voice terrifyingly calm. "I think we got the shot."

"Did it capture the anointing?" Bernice asked hopefully.

"It captured the butter, Bernice. It captured the butter."

Later that evening, Leroy sat at his computer in the den. He had spent an hour carefully cleaning butter out of his charging port with a toothpick. Now, the footage was loaded onto his screen.

He watched it. He watched the bad takes. He watched the "violent rolling pin" incident. And he watched the final take—the beautiful speech about "waiting," followed immediately by the flour explosion and the camera's death-dive into the butter.

He started to cut. He started to splice. He added a beat underneath it— something playful, a little jazzy piano loop.

He kept the mistake. He kept the flour cloud. He even kept the sound of the phone hitting the butter, adding a cartoon *SPLASH* sound effect.

"Bernice!" he called out. "Come here."

Bernice walked in, looking sheepish. "Is it ruined? Did I ruin your career as a cinematographer?"

"Watch," he said.

He played the video. It was ninety seconds long. It was chaotic. It was messy. But it was hilarious. And right in the middle, there was that thirty seconds of genuine wisdom that made your chest ache a little.

Bernice watched herself disappear into the flour cloud. She laughed. She laughed until she had to lean on Leroy's shoulder.

"Look at me," she wheezed. "I look like a ghost baker."

"It's gold," Leroy said. "Tasha, upload it."

Tasha, lurking in the doorway, gave a thumbs up. "Posting to TikTok and YouTube now. Hashtag #CinnamonRollDevotions #ButterFingers."

"You think people will watch it?" Bernice asked, wiping a tear. "I didn't even get to the

scripture."

"Bernice," Leroy said, kissing her forehead. "You *are* the scripture. You're a living epistle. Just... a very messy one."

Bernice smiled, watching the view count tick from 0 to 1.

"Well," she said, straightening her robe. "If the Lord can use a donkey, surely He can use a buttery phone."

"Amen," Leroy said. "Now go clean my kitchen."

Chapter 9

The Order That Broke the Camel's Back

Viral fame does not sound like applause. It sounds like a relentless, digital mosquito buzzing in your pocket.

Ding. Ding. Ding. Ding.

Tasha's phone had been vibrating off the table for six hours straight. The "Flour Cloud" video had hit 50,000 views overnight. By lunch the next day, it was at 200,000. People loved the wisdom about letting dough rise. But mostly, they loved watching Sister Bernice accidentally assault a bag of flour and hearing Leroy's deadpan "I think we got the shot" at the end.

But with the views came the comments. And with the comments came the DMs. And with the DMs came the orders.

"Mommom," Tasha said, scrolling through her iPad with wide eyes. "You have an order for six jars of Touch By Greatness from a lady in Nebraska. And a request for two dozen cinnamon rolls from a man in... is 'Llanfairpwllgwyngyll' a real place?"

"If they have a mailbox, we ship it to them!" Bernice shouted from the kitchen. She was currently wearing two aprons, one over the other, like a suit of armor. "Wales needs Jesus and sugar just like everybody else!"

The kitchen was no longer a kitchen. It was a disaster zone. The "Spice Zone" on Leroy's subwoofer had expanded. There were now fifty-pound bags of flour stacked against the refrigerator. The dining room table was buried under cardboard boxes. The smell of vinegar and yeast was so strong that the neighbors probably got a buzz just walking by the open window.

Leroy stood in the doorway, holding a piece of paper. He looked at Bernice. He looked like a man who had just survived a war, only to find out the enemy had reinforcements.

"Bernice," he said, his voice tight. "I just got off the phone with the credit card company. They

wanted to know if our card had been stolen because there are twelve charges to 'Bulk Honey Depot' in the last forty-eight hours."

"Tell them it's an investment!" Bernice yelled over the roar of her industrial mixer (which she had borrowed from the church kitchen without technically asking). "We have to spend money to make money, Leroy!"

"We are spending *my* retirement money, Bernice! This house is full of glass jars and sticky fluids! I can't find my car keys because you used the key bowl to mix the glaze!"

"Check the fruit basket!" she directed, not breaking her rhythm.

Then, the phone rang. The landline. The one that only telemarketers and serious people used. Bernice wiped her hands on her apron. "Answer that, Leroy. It might be Oprah."

"It's not Oprah, Bernice." Leroy picked up the receiver. "Hello? ... Yes, this is the residence of Sister Bernice. ... Who? ... The Tri-State Women of Destiny Conference?"

Bernice dropped a tray of rolls. *Clang.* Her eyes went wide. The Women of Destiny Conference was the Super Bowl of church ladies. It was hats, heels, and thousands of potential customers.

Leroy listened, his face paling. "Uh-huh. For this Saturday? ... Five hundred? ... Ma'am, that's in three days. ... Yes, I know she's 'anointed,' but she only has one oven."

He listened for another moment, then covered the mouthpiece. "Bernice. They want three hundred jars of dressing and two hundred cinnamon rolls for the welcome bags. By Friday night."

"Tell them yes!" Bernice screamed, doing a little dance that sent flour flying. "Tell them yes and amen!"

"Bernice, we can't—"

"TELL THEM YES, LEROY! THIS IS THE BREAKTHROUGH!"

Leroy sighed, defeated by the sheer force of her will. "She says... yes. We will deliver." He hung up the phone and looked at her. "You realize we are going to die, right? This is how we go. Buried under an avalanche of unbaked dough."

"Have faith, old man!" Bernice was already grabbing a notepad. "Call the boys. Call Darlene. Call the grandkids. All seventeen of them. If they can walk, they can work."

The next forty-eight hours were a blur of madness.

The house became a sweatshop. Darlene showed up, complaining the entire time but folding

boxes with terrifying speed. "I better get a tax write-off for this, Bernice. My manicure is ruined."

The brothers—Earl, James, and David—arrived for the promised barbecue, only to be handed aprons and put on "heavy lifting" duty, moving crates of jars from the garage to the kitchen.

"I thought we were tasting ribs," Earl grumbled, hauling a sack of sugar. "You're tasting the sweet satisfaction of family unity," Bernice barked. "Keep moving!"

The oven didn't turn off. It ran so hot that the kitchen temperature hovered around ninety degrees. Leroy had set up huge box fans in the windows, but it just blew hot air and cinnamon scent around.

By Friday afternoon, they were close. But cracks were showing.

They ran out of cinnamon. Real, high-quality cinnamon. Bernice refused to use the cheap stuff. "Go to the store, Leroy!"

"I went to the store three times today, Bernice! The manager thinks I have a problem!"

Then, the honey ran dry. The golden bear was squeezed until it wheezed, sputtering out one final drop.

"We need more honey!" Bernice cried, scraping the bottom of a mixing bowl.

"We are out," Tasha reported from the inventory station (the living room floor). "And the store is closed."

Bernice slumped against the counter. She was exhausted. Her hair was frizzy from the humidity. Her apron was stiff with dried dough. Her feet were throbbing in her slippers.

She looked at the order list. They were fifty jars short.

"I failed," she whispered. The energy finally drained out of her. "I took the order, and I can't fill it. The Women of Destiny are going to have dry salads. I'm a fraud."

The kitchen went silent. Even the mixer stopped whirring. The grandkids stopped labeling.

Leroy looked at his wife. He saw the slump in her shoulders. He saw the genuine fear in her eyes—not fear of losing money, but fear of failing her "calling."

He looked at the clock. 6:00 PM.

He looked at his car keys, which he had finally recovered from the fruit basket.

"How much honey do you need?" Leroy asked quietly.

Bernice looked up. "Gallons, Leroy. We need the big jugs."

Leroy grabbed his keys. "I know a guy."

"You know a guy for honey?" Darlene asked, raising an eyebrow.

"I know a guy who runs a bakery in the city," Leroy corrected. "He owes me a favor for fixing his sound system. Keep the oven hot."

He turned to leave, but stopped at the door. He looked at Bernice. "We aren't failing, Bernice. We're just... remixing the schedule. I'll be back in an hour."

Bernice watched him go. A lump formed in her throat.

"Alright!" she shouted, clapping her hands to break the tension. "You heard the man! Keep the oven hot! Tasha, check the rolls! Malik, stop eating the inventory! We are in overtime!"

When Leroy returned forty-five minutes later, he didn't just have honey. He had five gallons of premium clover honey and a professional-grade dough proofer he'd borrowed from the back of his friend's van.

"Don't ask," Leroy said, hauling the heavy equipment in. "Just bake."

They worked through the night. At 3:00 AM, Leroy was in the kitchen, washing dishes because they had run out of clean bowls. Bernice was labeling jars with shaky hands. The grandkids had long since passed out on the living room floor, sleeping in a pile of bubble wrap.

At 5:00 AM, the last box was taped shut.

Three hundred jars. Two hundred rolls.

Bernice sat down on a kitchen stool. She couldn't feel her legs. She looked at the wall of boxes stacked by the back door.

Leroy leaned against the sink, drying a metal bowl. He looked just as wrecked as she did. "We did it," Bernice whispered.

"We did it," Leroy agreed. He walked over and stood in front of her. "But Bernice?" "Yes, baby?"

"If you ever... and I mean *ever*... take an order like this again without consulting the Operations Manager—that's me—I am going to divorce you. I will file the papers. I will cite 'Irreconcilable

Differences due to Sticky Conditions.'"

Bernice chuckled, a tired, rasping sound. She leaned her head against his stomach, wrapping her arms around his waist.

"Deal," she murmured. "But Leroy?"

"Yeah?"

"Did you see those boxes? That's Greatness, Leroy. We touched Greatness."

Leroy looked at the boxes. He looked at his sleeping grandkids. He looked at his wife, covered in flour and smelling like a cinnamon factory explosion.

"Yeah," he said softly, resting his hand on her hair. "I guess we did. Now go to bed, woman. I'll load the truck."

Chapter 10

"I Don't Know What I'm Doing" Spaghetti

Saturday evening arrived with a sound that Sister Bernice had almost forgotten existed: Silence.

The "Women of Destiny" order had been delivered. The three hundred jars were gone. The cinnamon rolls were gone. The grandkids, clutching their hard-earned cash and smelling vaguely of vinegar, had been picked up by their parents.

Bernice lay on the living room couch, staring at the ceiling fan. She was currently unable to move. Her arms felt like lead. Her feet felt like they were two sizes too big for her body. She was wearing her robe, which was still dusted with flour from the night before, but she didn't care. If the Lord wanted to take her now, He would just have to accept a dusty angel.

She had slept for six hours straight—a nap of biblical proportions. Now, as she blinked awake, she realized two things.

First, she was alive.

Second, she was starving.

But the thought of standing up, walking to the kitchen, and lifting a pan was physically painful. She groaned, closing her eyes again. "Lord, send a raven with a sandwich. Or just a pizza delivery angel."

Then, she smelled it.

It wasn't cinnamon. It wasn't sugar. It wasn't the sharp tang of salad dressing. It was garlic. And onions. And something... meaty.

Bernice turned her head. Through the archway, she could see movement in the kitchen. Leroy.

He was standing at the stove, wearing one of her floral aprons, which looked ridiculous tied around his broad chest. He was holding a wooden spoon like a conductor's baton, muttering to himself.

Bernice watched him for a moment, a smile touching her tired lips. She summoned the strength to sit up and shuffle into the kitchen.

"What are you doing, old man?" she rasped, her voice still thick with sleep.

Leroy jumped, nearly dropping the spoon. "Bernice! You're up. I thought you were in a coma. I was about to check your pulse."

"I was resting my eyes," she said, leaning against the doorframe for support. "What is that smell?"

"That," Leroy announced, gesturing to a large pot bubbling on the stove, "is a masterpiece in progress. You cooked for five hundred people yesterday. Today, the kitchen is mine."

Bernice walked over and peered into the pot. It was a deep red sauce, thick and bubbling ominously. There were chunks of peppers, onions, mushrooms, and ground beef swirling in the vortex.

"It's spaghetti," Leroy clarified, stirring it aggressively. "Or at least, it's going to be. I call it 'I Don't Know What I'm Doing' Spaghetti."

"That's a confident title," Bernice teased.

"It's an honest title," Leroy corrected. "I looked for a recipe, but I couldn't find one that spoke to me. So I did a Bernice. I just started throwing things in."

Bernice raised an eyebrow. "You vibed it?"

"I vibed it," he nodded solemnly. "I found some garlic powder. Some Italian seasoning. A little bit of that red wine you use for 'medicinal purposes.' And... a secret ingredient."

"Leroy, if you put Touch By Greatness in this sauce, I'm calling the police."

"No dressing," he promised. "I put a pinch of brown sugar. To cut the acidity. I saw it on a cooking show once while I was waiting for my football game to start."

Bernice watched him. He looked focused. He looked capable. He was the man who had stayed up until 5:00 A.M. washing dishes so she could finish labeling. He was the man who had called

in a favor for honey. And now, he was trying to feed her.

"Sit down," Leroy ordered, pointing his spoon at the kitchen table. "Don't touch anything. You are on administrative leave."

Bernice sat. She watched him boil the noodles. She watched him drain them (escaping only a minor steam burn). She watched him toss the noodles into the sauce, mixing it all together until every strand was coated in red.

He scooped a mountain of pasta onto a plate, dusted it with enough parmesan cheese to simulate a blizzard, and placed it in front of her.

"Bon appétit," he said, sitting down with his own plate. "If it's terrible, we order pizza." Bernice picked up her fork. She twirled a massive bite. She blew on it. She took a bite. She chewed. She paused. She chewed again.

Her eyes widened.

"Leroy," she said, her mouth full.

"It's bad, isn't it?" Leroy sighed, reaching for his phone. "I knew it. Too much oregano. I'll call Domino's."

"Put the phone down," Bernice commanded. She took another bite, closing her eyes. "Leroy, this is... this is anointed."

"Stop playing."

"I'm serious. The brown sugar? Genius. It's savory, it's sweet, it's... it's the best thing I've eaten in weeks."

And she meant it. Maybe it was the exhaustion. Maybe it was the hunger. But the spaghetti was rich and comforting, a warm blanket for her stomach. It tasted like love. It tasted like someone else taking care of things for a change.

Leroy watched her eat, a look of immense satisfaction spreading across his face. He took a bite of his own.

"You know," he mumbled, "it actually isn't bad. I might have a future in this. *Chef Leroy's Beats and Eats*."

They ate in silence for a few minutes, the only sound the clinking of forks against plates. It was the companionable silence of two people who had been to war together and survived.

"We did good, didn't we?" Bernice asked softly, wiping sauce from her lip.

"We did good," Leroy agreed. "But Bernice, I meant what I said. No more surprises. My heart can't take it. And my car shocks can't take hauling five gallons of honey."

"I know," Bernice promised. "I think... I think I learned something this time. I need to pace myself. Rome wasn't built in a day, and neither is a dressing empire."

"Exactly," Leroy said. "Take your time. Let it rise. Like the dough."

Bernice smiled at him. "You were listening to my video."

"I edited the video, Bernice. I've heard that speech forty times. It's stuck in my head." He reached across the table and took her hand. His palm was rough, warm, and comforting.

"You're a force of nature, Bernice," he said quietly. "I make fun of you. I tease you about the handbags and the garden tools. But I'm proud of you. You saw something, and you made it happen. That's real."

Bernice felt tears prick her eyes. She squeezed his hand. "I couldn't do it without you, Leroy. You're my rhythm section. I'm just the melody. Without the beat, I'm just drifting."

"Yeah, well," Leroy cleared his throat, pulling his hand back to take another bite of spaghetti. "Just remember that when I buy those new studio monitors next week."

Bernice laughed, a full, hearty laugh that made her ribs ache. "Don't push your luck, old man. Eat your spaghetti."

"Yes, ma'am."

They finished their meal, scraping the plates clean. The kitchen was a mess again—sauce splatters on the stove, flour still in the corners—but neither of them moved to clean it.

Tonight, the dishes could wait. Tonight, they were just Bernice and Leroy. Full, tired, and happy.

"Hey," Leroy said, standing up and stretching. "You want to go watch TV? I think there's a rerun of *Shark Tank* on."

Bernice groaned as she stood up. "Oh, I love *Shark Tank*. I need to take notes. I'm going to pitch them next season."

Leroy froze. "Bernice. No."

"I'm just saying! Mr. Wonderful would love Touch By Greatness!"

"Bernice, walk to the living room. Do not pass Go. Do not collect two hundred dollars." She laughed and leaned into him as they walked out of the kitchen.

"Fine," she whispered. "But you know I'm right."

"I know," he sighed, wrapping an arm around her. "That's what I'm afraid of."

Chapter 11

Touching Greatness

Success tastes like many things. For some, it tastes like champagne. For others, it tastes like steak. For Sister Bernice, success tasted like a fresh cup of coffee drunk at 10:00 A.M. on a Monday, knowing she didn't have to answer to anyone but the Lord and the UPS delivery man.

The "Women of Destiny" conference had been a smash hit.

Bernice sat at the kitchen table—which was finally visible again after the Great Box purge—scrolling through her emails on her iPad. Tasha sat opposite her, managing the "Bernice Enterprises" social media accounts, a job she had officially accepted in exchange for a 5% commission and exemption from doing dishes.

"Listen to this one, Leroy," Bernice beamed, adjusting her reading glasses. "Sister Patty from Oklahoma writes: 'Dear Sister Bernice, I put *Touch By Greatness* on my husband's dry turkey meatloaf. He ate three slices. I believe this dressing has saved my marriage. Hallelujah.'"

Leroy, who was leaning against the counter eating a leftover cinnamon roll, chuckled. "That's a powerful testimony. You should put that on the bottle. 'Saves Marriages and Turkey.'"

"I just might," Bernice noted. "Oh, and here's another one from Pastor Stevens. 'The cinnamon rolls were a revelation. The dressing is a mystery. When can we order for the Men's Retreat?'"

"Tell him the Men's Retreat price is double," Leroy advised. "Men eat more."

"Mommom," Tasha interrupted, looking up from her phone. "The reviews are great. People are posting pictures of the jars everywhere. One lady took a selfie with the dressing at the Grand Canyon. I don't know why, but engagement is up 400%."

"Because Greatness travels, Tasha," Bernice said simply.

"But," Tasha continued, frowning slightly as she tapped her screen. "There's something else happening in the comments of the 'Flour Cloud' video."

Bernice froze. "Is it negative? Are they making fun of my hat? I knew that hat was too

architectural for TikTok."

"No, it's not the hat," Tasha said. "It's the audio."

"The audio?" Leroy perked up. "I fixed the audio. I balanced the levels."

"They love the audio, PopPop," Tasha said, turning the screen toward him. "Look at these comments."

Leroy walked over and squinted at the scrolling text.

User789: "Okay, the grandma is funny, but that BEAT drops hard. Who produced that?" MusicMan_22: "Is that a sample or original? The piano loop is smooth. Need the link." Holy Ghost Rider: "I came for the cinnamon rolls, stayed for the Lo-Fi Christian Hip Hop. Where can I download this track?"

DJ_Saved: "Yo, @BerniceEnterprises, tell your sound guy he's fired. Let's collab." Leroy stared at the screen. He blinked. He took off his glasses, wiped them on his shirt, and put them back on. The comments were still there.

"They... they like the beat?" Leroy asked, his voice quiet.

"They don't like it, Leroy," Bernice said, reading over his shoulder. "They love it. Look at this one: 'Can I get a bottle of dressing that comes with a mixtape?'"

Leroy looked up, a slow, bewildered smile spreading across his face. "A mixtape? With salad dressing?"

"It's a bundle deal!" Bernice shouted, slamming her hand on the table. "I see it now! *Feast for the Body, Beats for the Soul!*"

Leroy shook his head, laughing in disbelief. "I just threw that loop together to cover up the sound of you hitting the flour bag. It was background noise."

"There are no accidents in the Kingdom, Leroy!" Bernice declared. "You thought you were just covering up my mess, but you were laying down a masterpiece! You're viral, old man! You're trending!"

Leroy looked at Tasha. "Am I trending?"

"You're trending, PopPop," Tasha confirmed. "People are using the sound bite for their own videos. There's a challenge going around where people try to bake while dancing to your beat. It's called the #BerniceBoogie."

"Oh no," Leroy groaned, hiding his face in his hands. "I don't want to see people boogie."

"Too late," Bernice said. "You're famous. You're Leroy the Beatmaker. Just like you said."

The reality of it settled over the kitchen. For years, Leroy had sat in his den, headphones on, making music for an audience of one. He had supported Bernice's wild dreams, hauled her boxes, and tasted her experiments, all while his own passion hummed quietly in the background.

And now, the world was listening.

"Well," Leroy said, straightening up and adjusting his apron (he had forgotten to take it off). "If they want beats, I guess I better give them beats. I have a whole folder of tracks I haven't finished."

"Finish them!" Bernice commanded. "Tasha, put a link on the website. 'Music by DJ Leroy.' No, 'Producer L-Roy.' That sounds more hip."

"Please don't call me L-Roy," he begged.

"We'll workshop the name," Bernice conceded. "But this is it, Leroy. We're a team. A multimedia empire. I feed them; you make them dance. It's perfect."

Later that afternoon, the house was buzzing with a new kind of energy. Bernice was in the kitchen, packing a small order of ten jars for a local boutique. Leroy was in the den, but the door was open. The music was cranked up a little louder than usual.

Bernice paused in her packing to listen. It was a new track. Upbeat, funky, full of life. It sounded like a celebration.

She walked to the doorway of the den. Leroy was nodding his head, hands flying over his keyboard. He looked younger. He looked lighter.

"Hey!" she called out over the music.

Leroy turned down the volume. "Yeah? You need more honey?"

"No," she smiled, leaning against the frame. "I just wanted to say... I told you so." "You told me what?"

"I told you were good. I told you that you just needed patience. You waited, Leroy. And now look at you. Touching greatness."

Leroy spun his chair around. He looked at his wife—the woman who had driven him crazy for eighteen years with her schemes, the woman who had filled his house with boxes and his life with laughter.

"We're touching it together, B," he said softly. "It's a duet."

"A duet," she agreed. "Now, turn that back up. I have to mop the floor, and I can't mop without a rhythm."

Leroy laughed and cranked the volume.

As the bass kicked in, shaking the pictures on the walls, Sister Bernice grabbed her mop. She didn't just clean; she danced. She waltzed with the mop handle, spinning around the kitchen island, fueled by caffeine, success, and the sweet sound of her husband's music.

They had survived the launch. They had survived the "Women of Destiny." They had survived the flour explosion.

And as for what came next? Well, Bernice had an idea about a franchise, and Leroy had an idea about an album.

But for now, they were just Bernice and Leroy, dancing in the kitchen of a house built on love, faith, and a whole lot of cinnamon.

End of Book 1

About the Author

Koryn Philo is a writer and author of the newly released *The Adventures of Sister Bernice*. This marks her second published book—a milestone she credits to her unwavering faith in God and her personal resilience. Koryn writes from the heart, inspired and supported by her family.